I Don't Care
Said Big Bear

D0490404

'I Don't Care Said Big Bear'
An original concept by Katie Dale
© Katie Dale

Illustrated by Kathryn Selbert

Published by MAVERICK ARTS PUBLISHING LTD

Studio 3A, City Business Centre, 6 Brighton Road,

Horsham, West Sussex, RH13 5BB

© Maverick Arts Publishing Limited August 2018

+44 (0)1403 256941

A CIP catalogue record for this book is available at the British Library.

ISBN 978-1-84886-368-2

www.maverickbooks.co.uk

BRENT LIBRARIES	
KIN	
91120000381224	
Askews & Holts	07-Sep-2018
JF BEGINNER READER	£5.99

Blue

This book is rated as: Blue Band (Guided Reading)
This story is decodable at Letters and Sounds Phase 4/5.

I Don't Care Said Big Bear

by **Katie Dale**
illustrated by **Kathryn Selbert**

Big Bear was drifting off to sleep when...

Help! I'm stuck!

"I don't care," said Big Bear.

"It's not my problem."

She was drifting off

to sleep again when...

"I don't care," said Big Bear.

"It's not my problem."

She had just drifted off

to sleep when...

"I don't care," said Big Bear.

"It's not my problem."

She had just started snoring when...

CRACK!

Big Bear started to shiver.

She was freezing!

But just then...

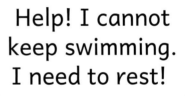

Help! I cannot keep swimming. I need to rest!

Big Bear was still freezing.

But she took Little One back

to his mum.

All the animals were glad to see them.

"I am," said Big Bear, shivering.

"B-but that's not your p-problem."

"You are right," the animals agreed.

"But we don't care!"

Quiz

1. What does Big Bear say?
a) Yippee
b) Oh well
c) I don't care

2. What happens to the baby puffin?
a) He falls out of his nest
b) He goes swimming
c) He needs food

3. What noise does the iceberg make?
a) Smash!
b) Boom!
c) Crack!

4. Who does Big Bear help?

a) A baby seal

b) A fish

c) A whale

5. Big Bear is...

a) Hot

b) Freezing

c) Boiling

Turn over for answers

Book Bands for Guided Reading

Pink

Red

Yellow

Blue

Green

Orange

Turquoise

Purple

Gold

White

The Institute of Education book banding system is a scale of colours that reflects the various levels of reading difficulty. The bands are assigned by taking into account the content, the language style, the layout and phonics.

Maverick Early Readers are a bright, attractive range of books covering the pink to purple bands. All of these books have been book banded for guided reading to the industry standard and edited by a leading educational consultant.

To view the whole Maverick Readers scheme, visit our website at

www.maverickearlyreaders.com

Or scan the QR code above to view our scheme instantly!

Quiz Answers: 1c, 2a, 3c, 4a, 5b